Pony-4-Sale

Do you love ponies? Be a Pony Pal!

Look for these Pony Pal books:

#1 I Want a Pony
#2 A Pony for Keeps
#3 A Pony in Trouble
#4 Give Me Back My Pony
#5 Pony to the Rescue
#6 Too Many Ponies
#7 Runaway Pony
#8 Good-bye Pony
#9 The Wild Pony
Super Special #1 The Baby Pony
#10 Don't Hurt My Pony
#11 Circus Pony
#12 Keep Out, Pony!
#13 The Girl Who Hated Ponies
#14 Pony-sitters
Super Special #2 The Story of Our Ponies
#15 The Blind Pony
#16 The Missing Pony Pal
Super Special #3 The Ghost Pony
#17 Detective Pony
#18 The Saddest Pony
#19 Moving Pony
#20 Stolen Ponies
#21 The Winning Pony
#22 Western Pony
#23 The Pony and the Bear
#24 The Unlucky Pony
#25 The Lonely Pony
#26 The Movie Star Pony
#27 The Pony and the Missing Dog
#28 The Newborn Pony
#29 Lost and Found Pony
#30 Pony-4-Sale

Coming Soon
#31 Ponies from the Past

Pony-4-Sale

Jeanne Betancourt

Illustrated by Paul Bachem

SCHOLASTIC INC.
New York Toronto London Auckland Sydney
Mexico City New Delhi Hong Kong

Acknowledgments

Thank you to Dr. Jayme Motler for her help with this story.

ISBN 0-439-16573-3

12 11 10 9 8 7 6 5 4 3 2 1   1 2 3 4 5 6/0

Printed in the U.S.A.
First Scholastic printing, April 2001

Contents

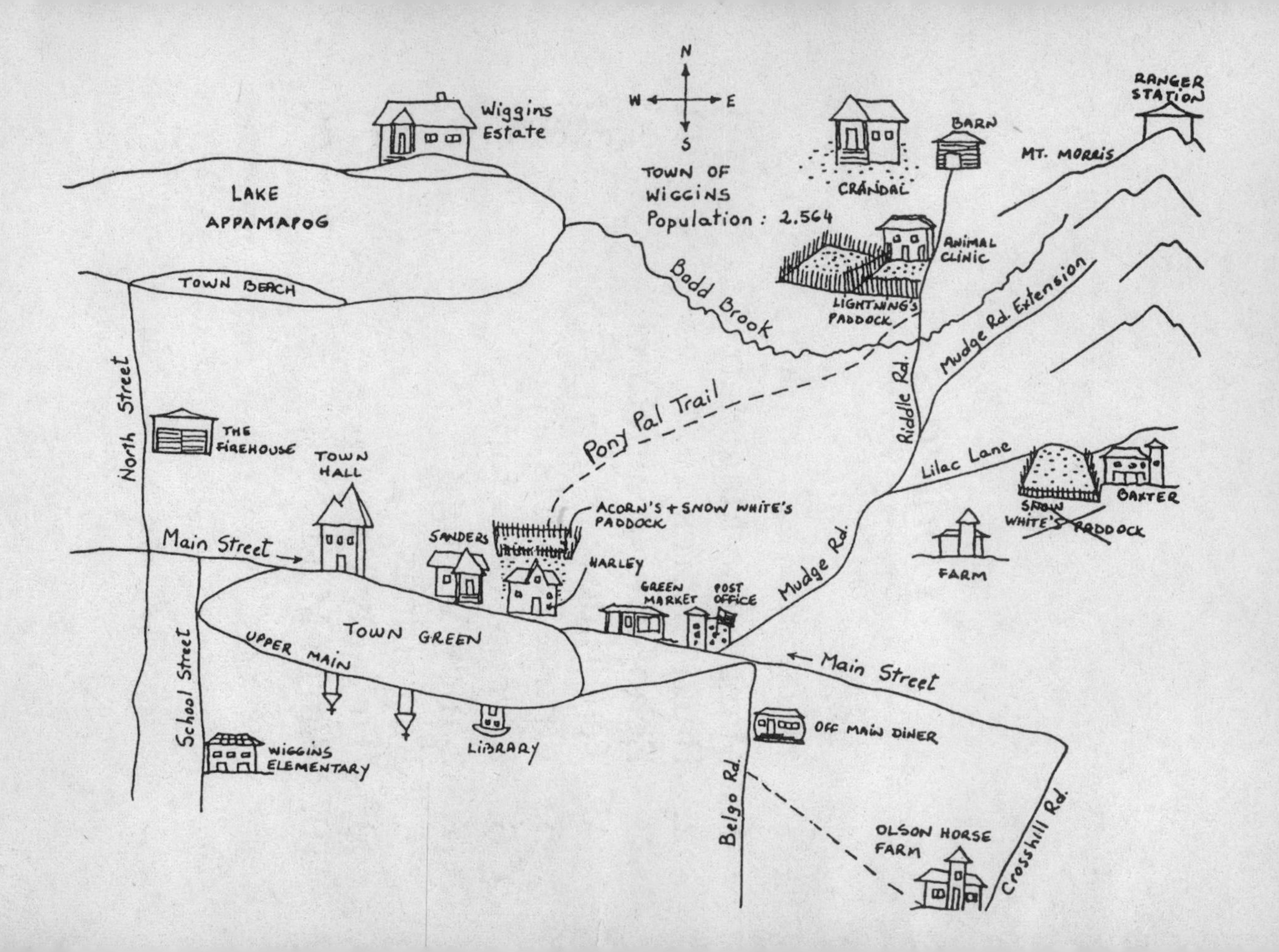
N
W
E
S
TOWN OF
WIGGINS
Population : 2.564
Wiggins
Estate
LAKE
APPAMAPOG
TOWN BEACH
CRANDAL
BARN
RANGER
STATION
MT. MORRIS
ANIMAL
CLINIC
LIGHTNING'S
PADDOCK
Badd Brook
Mudge Rd. Extension
Riddle Rd.
Pony Pal Trail
North Street
THE
FIREHOUSE
TOWN
HALL
Lilac Lane
BAXTER
SNOW
WHITE'S
PADDOCK
FARM
ACORN'S + SNOW WHITE'S
PADDOCK
SANDERS
HARLEY
Main Street
Mudge Rd.
GREEN
MARKET
POST
OFFICE
TOWN GREEN
UPPER MAIN
Main Street
School Street
WIGGINS
ELEMENTARY
LIBRARY
OFF MAIN DINER
Belgo Rd.
OLSON HORSE
FARM
Crosshill Rd.

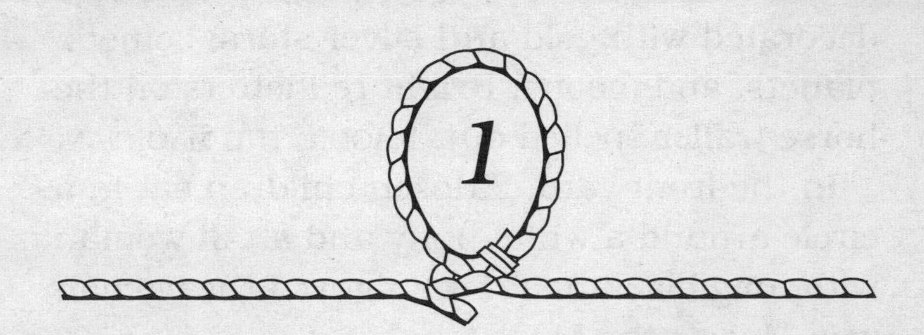

Maggie the Magician

Pam Crandal rode her pony along Mudge Road. She was going to meet her Pony Pals, Anna and Lulu, at Off-Main Diner. Anna's mother owned the diner. It was a favorite meeting place for the Pony Pals. Lightning trotted happily past houses and fields. Pam loved to go places on her pony.

Lightning stopped suddenly and turned. She was looking at a house across the road. The front porch of the house was decorated for a child's birthday party. Pam also noticed a pickup truck with a horse trailer parked out front. They were painted bright blue and decorated with gold and silver stars, comets, planets, and moons. Bright red letters on the horse trailer spelled out: MAGGIE THE MAGICIAN.

In the front yard, a dozen children sat in a circle around a white pony and a tall woman with long black hair. Pam figured the woman was Maggie the Magician.

A few adults watched the magic show from the porch.

Lightning whinnied softly.

"Okay, Lightning," Pam said as she dismounted. "Let's go check it out."

Pam led Lightning across the road and stopped at the fence. From there, they could see and hear the magic act. The white pony wore a big red-and-gold-checked ruffle around his neck. His saddle was decorated with gold stars. Maggie the Magician wore a bright blue tuxedo, a gold-colored top hat, and a red scarf.

Lightning's ears tipped forward and she sniffed the air. *Why is Lightning so interested in that white pony?* Pam wondered.

Does she think that he's Lulu's pony, Snow White?

"Are you ready for the next trick?" Maggie asked the children.

"Yes!" they shouted.

Maggie held out a big yellow hat and showed them the inside. "Is there anything in this hat?" she asked.

"No!" the children answered.

Maggie put the hat on the pony's head and held up her gold magic wand.

"What do we say to make magic happen?" she asked the children.

"Ab-ra-ca-da-bra and wow-wow kaaa-zoo!" they shouted.

Maggie waved the wand over the pony's head and lifted the hat. A small bird flew out and away.

The children cheered and clapped.

Pam watched the bird fly out of sight. I know how that trick works, she thought. There is a secret compartment with a trap-door in the hat. Maggie put the bird in there while no one was looking. When Maggie raises the hat, she opens the trapdoor to the secret compartment with her finger. Pam thought it wasn't a very nice trick. Not for the bird.

A little red-haired boy in the circle of children stood up. "Is it time for pony rides?" he asked. "Can we ride Cloud now?"

"Yes," answered Maggie. "And the birthday boy goes first."

As the little boy ran up to Cloud, a red-haired woman came off the porch.

"I'm going to ride the pony first, Mom," the boy called to her.

Maggie turned Cloud to line him up with the mounting step.

Cloud tossed his head and shied away.

Maggie yanked Cloud. He shook his head, but he didn't move forward.

The boy's mother pulled him away from the misbehaving pony. "I think we'll just skip the pony rides," she said.

Maggie waved her magic wand over Cloud. Water from the wand squirted in his face. "Bad pony," scolded Maggie. She said it in a

teasing voice, but she wasn't smiling. Pam could tell that Maggie was really angry at Cloud.

Maggie squirted Cloud again. He hung his head.

The children laughed.

Pam didn't think it was funny.

Lightning's ears twitched. She pawed the ground. Lightning doesn't like the way Maggie treats Cloud, either, thought Pam.

"Time for birthday cake!" shouted the boy's mother. "And party favors."

The children cheered as they ran to the porch.

The boy's mother shook Maggie's hand and thanked her.

"Sorry about the pony rides, Mrs. Gear," said Maggie. "I don't know what's gotten into Cloud lately."

"The magic show was great," said Mrs. Gear. "Maybe you don't need a pony for your act. You could use the children to help with tricks instead of a pony."

"Just what I've been thinking," agreed Maggie. "How would you like to buy a pony?"

"Not that one," laughed Mrs. Gear.

Mrs. Gear went back to the party on the porch. Maggie packed up her magician's props.

Pam wondered why Cloud wouldn't let the children ride him.

Maggie swung her bag of tricks over her shoulder, grabbed Cloud's lead rope, and led him toward the horse trailer.

Pam led Lightning over to meet them. She wanted to talk to Maggie about Cloud. When Cloud saw Lightning, he whinnied. The two ponies sniffed noses.

"Hi," said Pam. "I'm Pam Crandal. This is my pony, Lightning. Our ponies like each other."

"Good for them," said Maggie.

"Cloud's a nice-looking pony," continued Pam. "Have you had him for a long time?"

Maggie opened the horse trailer doors. She didn't answer Pam's question.

Pam looked into Cloud's eyes. She saw sadness there. And hurt. Poor pony, thought Pam. I want to help you.

"Why didn't Cloud let the children ride him?" Pam asked Maggie. "Has he done that before?"

Again, Maggie didn't answer. She slapped Cloud on the rump. Cloud lowered his head and walked slowly up the short ramp into the horse trailer.

Lightning nickered as if to say, "Hey, where are you going?"

Maggie lifted the ramp and slammed the door behind Cloud. "Useless animal," she muttered as she walked to the car.

The children on the porch were singing "Happy Birthday."

If I'm going to help Cloud I need some information, thought Pam. I don't even know where Maggie the Magician lives.

Maggie started the truck.

"Wait!" shouted Pam as she ran over to Maggie. "I liked your magic show. It's great. Do you do a lot of parties?"

"It's how I make my so-called living," answered Maggie.

"My brother and sister are five years old," Pam continued. "They're twins. And we might have a big birthday party for them. Do you have a business card? I'll give it to my parents."

Maggie smiled at Pam for the first time and handed her a business card. "Tell your parents I don't give pony rides anymore," she said. "No more pony. I'm selling him."

"What kind of a pony is he?" asked Pam.

"Are you going to buy him?" Maggie asked.

"I already have a pony," answered Pam.

Maggie leaned her head out the window and looked Lightning up and down.

"That looks like a well-behaved pony," she said.

"Lightning's great," said Pam proudly.

"Want to trade?" asked Maggie.

"No," answered Pam.

"Well, I don't blame you," she said. "Cloud's been a naughty pony lately. If I can't find a buyer soon, I'm going to sell him for the meat price."

Pam felt tears spring to her eyes. How could Maggie be so cruel? Just because Cloud was a little difficult, she was going to have him killed!

"Bye," Maggie said with a little wave.

Pam moved closer to Lightning as Maggie drove away with Cloud.

"That is a very mean lady," Pam told her pony.

Pam mounted Lightning and moved her into a trot. She was late for meeting her Pony Pals. She needed to tell them about Cloud. They had to find a buyer for the sad white pony!

Barn Chores

Pam rode Lightning up to the hitching post in front of Off-Main Diner. Snow White and Acorn were already there. The three ponies nickered and whinnied softly to one another. Pam wondered if Cloud had any pony friends. She didn't think so.

Pam went into the diner. Anna and Lulu were sitting in the Pony Pals' favorite booth.

"We're having grilled cheese sandwiches and chocolate milk shakes," Anna told Pam. "What do you want?"

"I'll have the same thing," answered Pam. "Sorry I'm late."

Anna went to the kitchen to put in their order.

While the three friends waited for their food, Pam told them about Cloud. She put Maggie's business card on the table where they could all see it.

MAGGIE THE MAGICIAN
Magic Tricks, Games, Balloons, Party Favors, ~~Pony Rides~~
Call: Margaret Sullivan at 555-9802
156 Belgo Road, Wiggins
PONY-4-SALE!

"Maggie lives on Belgo Road," said Lulu. "We're on Belgo Road right now."

"The diner's address is 5 Belgo Road," said Anna.

"So number 156 is probably near the other end," added Pam.

"Pony Pal meals on board!" shouted the cook. The girls went to the counter to pick up their sandwiches and milk shakes.

"Let's go to Maggie's after lunch," suggested Anna. "We'll help her find a good owner for Cloud."

"Maggie is very unfriendly — even mean," said Pam. "I don't think she'll talk to us unless *we're* going to buy him."

"Then one of us should *pretend* we want to buy a pony," said Lulu.

"That's a good idea," agreed Pam.

"Maggie already knows you have a pony, Pam," said Anna. "So one of us has to do it."

"Anna, it should be you," said Lulu. "You're the best actress."

"Perfect," agreed Pam. "Just don't let her know that you already have a pony."

Anna took a sip of her milk shake and looked up at her friends. "But you said she was mean, Pam."

"She won't be mean if she thinks you'll buy Cloud," said Pam. "And I'll go with you. I'll hide nearby. Be sure to ask her lots of questions."

"I'll stay on Belgo Road with our ponies,"

added Lulu. "We'll all be there. Only Maggie won't know it."

"Okay," agreed Anna. "How's this?" Anna put on a sweet smile. "Hello, Ms. Sullivan. My mommy and daddy said I could have a pony. I heard you have a pony for sale. Can I see it?"

"Bravo!" exclaimed Lulu.

"You are the best, Anna," added Pam.

While the girls finished lunch, they made up questions to ask Maggie.

"I'll be so nervous," said Anna. "I might not remember the answers."

Pam held up her little notebook. "I'll be right there," she reminded her friend. "And I'll take notes."

Soon the Pony Pals were riding their ponies to the end of Belgo Road. Anna and Acorn went first, then Lulu and Snow White. Pam and Lightning took up the rear.

As they rode, Pam thought about her Pony Pals.

Lulu was right. Of the three of them, Anna was the best actress. But Lulu knew the most about nature. Lulu Sanders's father was a naturalist who traveled all over the world studying wild animals. Her mother died when she was little. After that Lulu traveled with her father. But when Lulu turned ten, her father said she had to live in one place. Now she lived with her Grandmother Sanders in a house next door to Anna. Best of all, Acorn and Snow White shared a paddock behind Anna's house.

Anna Harley and Pam Crandal met the first day of kindergarten. During art period, Anna drew a pony. Pam admired Anna's drawing and told her she had her own pony. Anna was very impressed.

"You can ride my pony," five-year-old Pam told her new friend. "My mommy can teach you how."

Soon Anna was taking riding lessons at Mrs. Crandal's riding school. Pam's father was a veterinarian and had an animal clinic. There was always something exciting going on at the Crandals'.

Anna liked riding school much more than

regular school. She was dyslexic, so reading and math were hard for her. But Anna loved to draw and paint. Pam thought Anna was the best artist she knew.

Now Anna halted Acorn and dismounted. Lulu and Pam did the same. Anna pointed to a mailbox a few yards in front of them. The number 156 was printed on the side. A handmade sign stood next to the mailbox. The sign read: PONY-4-SALE.

A driveway led from the mailbox through the woods. But the girls couldn't see the house from the road.

Anna and Pam handed their ponies over to Lulu.

"Wish me luck," Anna said to Lulu.

"Good luck," Lulu told her.

Anna walked up the driveway. Pam sneaked through the woods near her. Soon the two girls saw a house and a small fenced-in paddock with a pony shed. Bushes lined the yard on one side.

Pam pointed to the bushes. "I'll hide over there," she whispered to Anna.

While Anna went to the house to look for Maggie, Pam sneaked over to her hiding place.

From there, Pam could see Anna knocking on the front door. She also saw Cloud standing in the little paddock. He looked lonely.

A minute later, Maggie and Anna walked into the paddock. Anna went up to Cloud. Now Pam could hear their conversation. Maggie was being very nice to Anna. She's only being nice because she thinks Anna might buy Cloud, thought Pam.

"He is such a pretty pony," Anna said. "Is he fun to ride?"

"Of course he is," said Maggie. "I'd ride him for you, but I'm too tall for a pony."

"What kind of a pony is Cloud?" asked Anna.

"He is a Connemara pony," answered Maggie. "That's a wonderful breed. He was born in Ireland. An excellent stable brought him to America and trained him."

"What's the name of the stable?" asked Anna.

"Echo Farm," answered Maggie.

Pam couldn't believe her ears. Cloud was a Connemara, just like Lightning! They'd both been born in Ireland, and they'd both come to Echo Farm in America! How old is Cloud? wondered Pam.

Just then, Anna asked Maggie, "How old is Cloud?"

Pam smiled to herself. She loved it when the Pony Pals thought alike.

"Cloud is ten years old," Maggie told Anna. "That means he's mature, but not too old. I think he's a perfect pony for you."

Cloud is the same age as Lightning, thought Pam. They were probably at Echo Farm together.

Anna put her hand on Cloud's head and ran it down his cheek. Cloud pulled his head up. He didn't want Anna to touch him.

What is wrong with Cloud? wondered Pam. Why won't he let Anna touch him?

Echofarm@realnet.net

Pam's nose twitched. It was the start of a sneeze. If she sneezed, Maggie would find her spying. Pam pressed her finger against her upper lip. It stopped the sneeze. That was a close call, thought Pam.

"Why doesn't Cloud let me touch him?" Anna asked Maggie.

"Cloud is a shy pony," answered Maggie.

"I'm shy, too," said Anna in her sweet-little-girl actress voice.

"Are you going to tell your parents that you want to buy him?" asked Maggie.

"Yes," answered Anna.

Maggie walked Anna toward the driveway. Pam waited until Maggie went back into the house. While Anna walked on the driveway, Pam sneaked back through the woods.

Lulu and the ponies were waiting for them. Pam and Anna told Lulu what they learned about Cloud.

Suddenly, Anna put up her hand. "Shhh," she warned. "I hear a car."

Pam heard a car motor, too. It was coming from the direction of Maggie's place.

"Hurry," said Pam. "Hide. We don't want Maggie to see us together."

The three girls quickly moved into the woods with their ponies. Pam and Lightning went behind two big pine trees. From there, Pam saw Maggie drive by. When Maggie's car was out of sight, the Pony Pals came out of hiding.

"What next?" asked Lulu as she pulled pine needles out of Snow White's mane.

"I have to go home," said Pam as she mounted Lightning. "I have to do barn chores. The boy who was working for my mother went back to college."

"We'll help you," offered Anna.

"And have a Pony Pal meeting about Cloud while we do it," added Lulu.

Forty-five minutes later, the Pony Pals were in the Crandals' new barn.

They put the riding-school ponies and horses in the paddocks, cleaned out the stalls, put in fresh straw, and filled the hay nets and water buckets.

While they worked, they talked about Cloud.

"I think Lightning remembers Cloud from Echo Farm," concluded Pam.

Anna hung up a hay net. "Cloud looks skinny," she said. "He doesn't look healthy like Lightning."

"Did you see Cloud when you bought Lightning?" asked Lulu.

Pam leaned on the stall half-door. She thought back to the day she picked out Lightning. "There were a lot of ponies at Echo Farm," she told her friends. "Some of them were white. They all looked great. And they were all well trained." She sighed. "If Cloud really came from Echo Farm, he's been mistreated since then."

"That's so sad," said Anna.

"Let's e-mail Echo Farm," suggested Pam. "I know the owner, Mr. O'Connor. He can tell us if Cloud really was there. Maybe he'll know where Cloud went next."

"Three helpers!" a woman's voice exclaimed. "How wonderful."

Pam's mother was walking toward them. She looked at each of the clean stalls. "Thank you, girls," she said. "You've done a great job." She smiled at Anna and Lulu. "Can you two have dinner with us tonight?" she asked. "We're having spaghetti and meatballs. Then you can have a barn sleepover."

"And help Pam with the chores again in the morning," added Anna with a giggle.

"It's a *perfect* idea," agreed Pam.

"Girls, I'm sorry there's so much to do right now," said Mrs. Crandal. "I'm looking for new stable help. Meanwhile, I'm very grateful to the Pony Pals."

"Do you need another school pony, Mrs. Crandal?" asked Lulu. "A really pretty white pony."

"You're not selling Snow White, are you?" asked Mrs. Crandal with alarm.

"Oh, no," answered Lulu. "This is a different white pony. His name is Cloud."

Anna and Pam exchanged a glance. Lulu was trying out an idea they hadn't discussed. That was against the Pony Pal rules.

"Pam said he's really cute," added Lulu.

"No more ponies," exclaimed Mrs. Crandal. She looked at her watch. "I have to get ready for a riding lesson."

Mrs. Crandal left.

"Why did you ask my mother to buy Cloud?" Pam asked Lulu.

"I thought it was a good idea," said Lulu.

"You should have talked to Pam and me about it first," put in Anna. "It's a Pony Pal rule."

"You asked her at the worst time," added

Pam. "My mother needs someone to take care of ponies, not another pony to take care of."

"It's no big deal," said Lulu. "She said no."

Pam felt annoyed with Lulu. Breaking a Pony Pal rule *was* a big deal. The three Pony Pals always talked about their solutions for Pony Pal problems. They had to agree on an idea before they tried it.

After the girls finished cleaning the stables, they went to the barn office. It was time to e-mail Mr. O'Connor. Pam turned on the computer.

"You type, Pam," said Anna.

"And we'll *all* decide what to say," added Lulu.

"Of course we will," said Pam sternly. "That's how the Pony Pals work."

Pam knew that she was being rude to Lulu. But she didn't say she was sorry. Why should I? thought Pam. Lulu didn't say she was sorry, either.

Pam tried to forget about being annoyed. She concentrated on writing the e-mail.

The three girls worked on it until they agreed that it was perfect.

Dear Mr. O'Connor:

I am Pam Crandal. I bought a pony from you. Her name is Lightning. I wrote to you once before and asked you a lot of questions about Lightning. You were very helpful. Now I want to ask you questions about another Connemara pony. The present owner says he's from Echo Farm. His name is Cloud and he is ten years old like Lightning. Did you sell Cloud to a Margaret Sullivan? (She is also known as Maggie the Magician.)

My Pony Pals and I don't think Ms. Sullivan treats Cloud very well. We want to help Cloud.

Thank you.

Sincerely,
Pam Crandal

P.S. Lightning acts like she knows Cloud. Were they at Echo Farm at the same time? Did Cloud come from Ireland on the plane with Lightning?

"I hope Mr. O'Connor checks his e-mail a lot," said Anna.

"Me, too," agreed Pam.

"I've never seen Cloud," said Lulu. "All I know is that he's white."

"I have an idea," said Anna. "Lulu, you should go to Maggie's and pretend you want to buy a pony. Like I did."

"Good idea," agreed Pam as she turned off the computer. "Then Maggie will think *two* people want to buy Cloud. That will give us more time to find a real buyer."

"Pam, you should go with Lulu," said Anna. "You know the most about ponies. You'll know what to ask Maggie."

"She doesn't like me," said Pam.

"She'll like you if you have a buyer for Cloud," said Anna.

"Okay," agreed Pam. "I'll go. And I'll bring Lightning. Cloud will like that. And we need to see how Cloud rides, too. That's important for finding a real buyer."

Pam took a couple of carrots from the tack room for Cloud and Lightning and stuck them in her pocket. The three girls saddled up their ponies. As Pam rode Lightning onto Riddle Road, she wondered what it would be like to ride Cloud.

4

Test Ride

The girls and their ponies stopped near Maggie's driveway.

"I'll stay here with Snow White and Acorn," said Anna. "Good luck."

Pam rode Lightning up Maggie's driveway. Lulu walked beside them.

"I see Maggie's truck," Pam told Lulu. "She must be here."

When they reached the end of the driveway, Lightning whinnied to Cloud. The white pony whinnied back and ran over to the fence.

Maggie came out of the house. "What are you doing here?" she asked when she saw Pam.

"I brought my friend Lulu Sanders," answered Pam. "She wants to buy a pony."

"A *white* pony," added Lulu.

"Have your parents said you can buy a pony?" asked Maggie.

"My father said I could," answered Lulu.

Maggie smiled. "How perfect," she said, "because I have a white pony to sell. But you have to act fast. You're not the only one who wants to buy Cloud."

Pam took the carrots out of her pocket and held them out for the ponies. Lightning chewed happily on hers. Cloud took a bite, spit it out, and turned his head away.

"How come Cloud doesn't like carrots?" asked Pam.

"He'll only eat his feed," said Maggie. "He's not spoiled, like some ponies."

Lulu and Pam exchanged a glance. Pam could tell that Lulu didn't like Maggie, either.

"Lulu wants to test-ride Cloud," Pam told Maggie.

"I don't let inexperienced riders on him," said Maggie. "You can take lessons after you buy him, Lulu."

"But she already knows how to ride," insisted Pam. "I let her ride Lightning all the time."

Maggie looked Lulu up and down. "Do you really know how to ride?" she asked.

"Yes," answered Lulu. "I'm a good rider."

"All right," agreed Maggie. "You can ride him."

Maggie went into the shed and came back with Cloud's tack.

"We can help you saddle him," suggested Pam.

"I'd rather do it myself," said Maggie.

Cloud backed up when Maggie put on the saddle. He shook his head when she put the bit in his mouth. And he puffed out his belly when Maggie tightened the girth.

Lulu tugged on Pam's sleeve. "He's acting

strange. Do you think he's safe to ride?" she whispered nervously.

"Sure," Pam whispered back. "Just be firm with him. Let him know that you're the boss."

Maggie turned to Lulu. "Well, he's ready to go."

"Go ahead," Pam told Lulu.

Maggie held Cloud while Lulu swung up into the saddle. I hope Cloud can't tell that Lulu is nervous, thought Pam.

Maggie handed Lulu the reins.

"Keep him at a walk," Pam instructed Lulu.

But Cloud didn't want to walk. He held his head up and ran across the paddock. He wouldn't turn or stop. He was running straight toward the fence!

"Rein him in!" Pam shouted to Lulu.

Cloud stopped with a jerk.

Lulu half jumped, half fell off. She looked frightened, but she wasn't hurt. Cloud shook his head.

Lightning pawed the ground nervously. "It's okay," Pam told Lightning in a soothing voice. "Everything is going to be okay."

"You pulled too hard on his mouth, Lulu," Maggie scolded. "Maybe you haven't ridden so much, after all."

"She hasn't," agreed Pam.

Lulu glared at Pam.

"So, do you still want to buy Cloud?" Maggie asked Lulu.

"Yes," answered Lulu. "He's a — a — nice pony."

"She'll take more lessons after she buys him," added Pam.

Maggie gave Lulu her business card. "Be sure your father calls," Maggie told Lulu. "Or someone else might buy Cloud first."

"Okay," Lulu agreed.

The girls said good-bye to Maggie and headed toward the driveway. Lightning looked over her shoulder and whinnied a good-bye to Cloud. Cloud whinnied back. Pam thought Cloud sounded sad.

Lulu walked ahead of Pam and Lightning.

"Well, that was a close call," Pam said to Lulu's back.

Lulu turned to her. "What do you mean?" she asked.

"I mean you could have gotten hurt," answered Pam.

"Because you told me to ride a dangerous animal!" said Lulu angrily.

"Shh," warned Pam. "Maggie will hear you."

They came to the end of the driveway. Anna was waiting for them.

"How did it go?" she asked. "What did you find out?"

"We don't have time to talk," answered Pam. "We have to get away from here. We don't want Maggie to see us together."

The three girls mounted their ponies and rode down Belgo Road.

"Did Lulu ride Cloud?" asked Anna.

"Not really," answered Pam.

Lulu halted Snow White and blocked Pam and Lightning's way. "You think that it was my fault?" she said.

"What happened?" asked Anna with alarm.

"Pam should know if a pony is safe to ride," said Lulu. "I trusted her."

"And I trusted you to know *how* to ride," Pam replied loudly.

"You're so smart about ponies," Lulu told Pam. "You knew it was dangerous for me to get on Cloud and you let me do it! You care more about solving Pony Pal problems than you do about your Pony Pals."

"Maybe you *did* pull too hard on his mouth!" shouted Pam.

A blue truck raced toward them. The girls moved their ponies to the side of the road. The truck slowed down as it passed. Maggie the Magician glared at all three Pony Pals and honked her horn.

Snow White whinnied nervously.

Lightning pawed the ground.

Acorn stood still and stared after the car.

The dust from the road blew up around them.

Whose Fault Is It?

"Well, Maggie saw us," said Pam. "Now she knows that we are all friends."

"I told her I didn't have a pony," said Anna, "and she saw me with one."

"I told her I wanted a white pony," added Lulu, "and she saw me riding one!"

"She knows you two aren't serious buyers," put in Pam.

"Now who is going to buy Cloud?" asked Lulu. "He behaves so badly."

"Maggie will sell him for the meat price," concluded Anna sadly.

"Let's go back to my place," suggested Pam. She looked at her watch. "We can have an emergency Pony Pal meeting before dinner."

"I'm not going to your house," said Lulu. "Or to your sleepover. I'm going home."

"Do what you want," snapped Pam.

"Please stop," pleaded Anna. "This Pony Pal problem is more important than your little fight."

"It isn't a *little* fight," Lulu told Anna. "Pam let me do something dangerous, and she doesn't even care."

Lulu turned Snow White around and galloped ahead.

"You should go after her," Anna told Pam.

"Why?" asked Pam. "I didn't know how hard Cloud was to ride. If I did, I wouldn't have let her ride him. She should know that."

"But —" began Anna.

"You can go with her if you want," said Pam.

"I'm coming with you," said Anna. "We

have to figure out what we can do for Cloud."

"So let's go," said Pam.

Pam started riding. Anna followed. They didn't talk until they reached the Crandals' barn.

Anna pulled Acorn up beside Lightning. "Maybe you should call Lulu," Anna told Pam, "and tell her you're sorry."

Pam dismounted. "I don't have anything to be sorry for," she said.

While Anna put the ponies in the paddock, Pam went to the barn office to check for e-mail. There was a message from Echo Farm!

"Mr. O'Connor wrote to us," she shouted out the window to Anna.

Anna ran into the office and Pam read her the e-mail.

Dear Pam Crandal:

Thank you for writing to me about Cloud. I am disturbed to learn that one of our ponies is not in a good home. Cloud was such a wonderful pony that I kept him for my own daughter. She rode him for a few years. When she went away to school, we decided to sell Cloud. But I did not sell Cloud to Maggie Sullivan. I sold Cloud to Gerald Young from Milton. The pony was for his son, and I think the son's name was Sandy. After receiving your e-mail, I called Mr. Young. But the Youngs no longer live in Milton. The telephone company gave me a number in Wiggins for them. When I called that number, no one answered. Since you live in Wiggins, perhaps you could investigate. The Youngs' new phone number is 555-7689.

Please let me know what happens. I am very concerned about Cloud.

Sincerely yours,

Richard O'Connor

"So Mr. O'Connor didn't sell Cloud to Maggie," said Pam. "But who is Sandy Young?"

"I don't know," grumbled Anna. "I've never

heard of him. Maybe he just moved here."

"Well, we need to find him," said Pam.

"Why?" asked Anna.

"Maybe he can tell us why Cloud behaves so badly. I wonder if that's why he sold him."

Anna frowned. Pam knew what she was thinking. Anna wanted her to make up with Lulu.

"If Lulu cared about Cloud she would be here," said Pam.

"It takes *three* Pony Pals to solve a problem," Anna reminded her. "You should call her."

"I'm calling Sandy Young first," Pam told Anna.

Pam dialed the Youngs' number, but no one answered.

As soon as Pam hung up the phone, it rang. Pam picked it up. It was Lulu. "I'd like to speak to Anna," Lulu said.

Pam handed Anna the phone. She stared at the computer screen and listened to Anna's end of the conversation.

Anna told Lulu about the e-mail from Mr.

O'Connor. Then she listened to something Lulu was saying.

"That's a great idea, Lulu," Anna said into the phone. "We'll do it right away." Finally, Anna hung up.

"Lulu's coming over," she told Pam. "But she still thinks you should apologize."

"I didn't do anything wrong," said Pam. "Besides, we have to save Cloud. That's most important."

"That's why Lulu's coming over," said Anna. "To help save Cloud even if you two are fighting. She already has a good idea."

"What is it?" asked Pam.

"That we should ask your father if he knows Cloud," answered Anna. "Maybe he took care of him."

"It's a good idea," admitted Pam. "I should have thought of it. If my father treated Cloud, he'll know a lot about him. He might even know why Cloud misbehaves."

"If we know why he misbehaves, it will be easier to find him a buyer," added Anna.

Anna and Pam ran over to Dr. Crandal's

clinic. A woman came out leading a Great Dane. She looked like she'd been crying. She smiled at Pam. "Your father saved my Mitzy's life," said the woman.

Pam felt proud of her father. I just hope we can save Cloud's life, too, she thought as she went into his office.

Dr. Crandal was standing at his desk. "Hi, girls," he said when they came in. "What's up?"

Pam explained that they had a Pony Pal problem and needed his help.

"Where's the third Pony Pal?" he asked. "Where's Lulu?"

Pam was quiet.

"She's on her way," said Anna.

Pam told her father all about Cloud.

"We wondered if you took care of him," added Anna.

"I don't remember a pony named Cloud. Or a magician," said Dr. Crandal. He turned to his computer. "But let's see if I have a file for him."

Pam and Anna looked over Dr. Crandal's

shoulder while he looked up the name Cloud. There was no record of a pony called Cloud. Next, he looked under the name Maggie Sullivan. He had a horse owner called Tim *O'*Sullivan, but no Maggie Sullivan.

"Look under the name Gerald Young," suggested Pam. "Maybe you took care of Cloud before Maggie bought him."

Dr. Crandal searched under the names of Gerald Young and Sandy Young. Finally, he looked up at Pam and Anna. "Sorry, girls," he said. "I never took care of Cloud."

"I don't think anyone has in a long time," said Pam. "Cloud is a neglected pony."

"Thank you, anyway, Dr. Crandal," said Anna sadly.

"Cheer up, Anna," said Dr. Crandal. "When the three Pony Pals work together, problems get solved."

Anna looked at Pam. Pam looked away. She wished she hadn't had a fight with Lulu. But it was too late now.

Reverse Directory

Pam and Anna waited for Lulu outside. Pam sat on the paddock fence and called to Lightning. When Lightning ran up to her, she stroked her pony's smooth cheek. She thought, Lightning and Cloud came from the same farm and they were trained together. Lightning is a happy, healthy pony. She likes me to ride her. What happened to Cloud? Why is he so unhappy and difficult?

"I wonder what Sandy Young is like," said Anna.

"Me, too," said Pam. "I wonder why he sold his pony. We need to find out."

Pam looked across the field and saw Lulu riding off Pony Pal Trail. The mile-and-a-half trail connected the Harleys' paddock with the Crandals' property. It was a great short-cut for the Pony Pals.

Lulu pulled Snow White up beside the paddock fence and dismounted. She ignored Pam.

"Did you talk to Dr. Crandal about Cloud?" Lulu asked Anna.

Anna nodded. "But he never treated Cloud," she said.

"Anna, how can we find out where the Youngs live?" asked Pam.

Anna shrugged her shoulders. "I don't know," she said.

"Anna, I have an idea about that," said Lulu. "We can use the reverse telephone directory on the computer. If you type in a phone number, it will tell you the address."

"That's a great idea," said Anna. "Let's try it."

Pam thought that Lulu's idea was great, too. But she didn't say so.

Pam jumped off the fence, and the three girls went back to the barn office.

"Tell Lulu she can use the computer," Pam whispered to Anna. "Since she knows how to use the reverse directory."

"Tell her yourself," Anna whispered back.

But Pam didn't have to tell Lulu. When they got to the office, Lulu sat down in front of the computer and turned it on. "I'll look up the Youngs' address," she said. "What's their phone number?"

Pam handed Anna a piece of paper with the Youngs' phone number. Anna handed Lulu the paper.

Lulu typed in several commands. Finally, the Youngs' address came up.

"Eighty-five School Street," Lulu read off the computer screen.

Pam checked her watch. It was already six-thirty. "It's almost dinnertime," she told Anna.

"Let's go to the Youngs' first thing tomorrow," Lulu told Anna. "If Pam agrees."

"Tell Lulu I agree with that plan," Pam told Anna.

"Stop it!" shouted Anna. "Both of you. This is such a stupid fight. I don't even know what you're fighting about anymore."

"She told me to ride a dangerous animal!" yelled Lulu.

"I didn't know that Cloud would be so hard to control!" shouted Pam.

The telephone rang and Pam answered it. It was her mother calling from the house to say dinner was ready.

Pam hung up the phone. "Tell Lulu that dinner is ready," she told Anna.

Anna laughed.

"What's so funny?" asked Lulu and Pam in unison.

"You two," said Anna. "It's the stupidest argument."

Pam sneaked a look at Lulu. At just that moment Lulu looked at Pam.

The corners of Lulu's mouth turned up in

a little smile. "Riding Cloud was like riding an unbroken pony in a western show," she said.

"But you held on," said Pam. "I would have fallen off. You must have been really scared."

"I was," admitted Lulu. "I guess that's why I got angry at you."

"I knew Cloud didn't like to be ridden," said Pam. "I shouldn't have let you ride him."

"I'm sorry," said Lulu and Pam in unison.

"I'm sorry I got mad at you before, too," said Pam. "When you asked my mom to buy Cloud."

"That's okay," said Lulu. "I'm sorry I broke a Pony Pal rule."

"I'm sorry, too," said Anna.

"What are *you* sorry about?" asked Pam.

"I'm sorry that I'm going to beat you two to the house!" she teased.

"Oh, no, you're not," said Pam.

The three friends went outside and lined up next to the barn door.

"On your mark," they chanted, "get set, go!"

The three friends ran side by side. No one was winning. Lulu and Pam exchanged a smile. It was great to be friends again.

Pam was happy the fight was over. But she was sad, too. Sad about Cloud.

"I just hope we can find a buyer for Cloud before it's too late," said Lulu.

"We'll find a way," said Anna. "Now that we're all working together."

I hope Anna's right, thought Pam.

The next morning, the Pony Pals rode their ponies through town to School Street. They stopped in front of 85 School Street. It was a four-story-high building with four mailboxes.

"There must be four apartments," said Lulu.

"I wonder which one the Youngs live in," said Pam.

"I'll stay with the ponies," offered Anna, "while you two do detective work."

The front door was unlocked, so Pam and Lulu walked in.

"Let's start on the top floor," suggested Lulu, "and work our way down." They went up to the fourth floor, knocked on the door, and waited.

"I hope the Youngs are nicer than Maggie the Magician," said Pam.

"Me, too," agreed Lulu.

No one answered the door.

"Are you looking for someone?" a woman's voice called up the stairs.

Pam looked over the railing. An elderly woman smiled up at her from the third floor.

"We're looking for the Youngs," Pam told the woman.

"They'd be at work," said the woman.

"What about Sandy Young?" asked Lulu.

"He's probably out," said the woman.

Pam and Lulu went down to the third floor. The woman told them that the Youngs had moved in the week before. And that Sandy Young was twelve years old.

"A nice young man," the woman said. "He

helps me carry up my groceries. He's looking for part-time work."

"Did he ever say anything about a pony?" asked Lulu. "A pony named Cloud?"

"No," answered the woman. "But he couldn't have a pony here, you know. It's an apartment building, and there's no yard for a pony."

Pam and Lulu thanked the woman and started down the stairs.

"We could ride around looking for him," Pam suggested to Lulu.

"Except we don't know what he looks like," said Lulu.

"Good point," agreed Pam.

Pam and Lulu reached the first floor and opened the front door.

A boy on a bike was talking to Anna.

Sandy Young

Anna introduced Pam and Lulu to the boy. He was Sandy Young.

"I hear my old pony lives in Wiggins," Sandy said cheerfully. "I didn't know that. I can't wait to see him again. Do you think the lady who owns him will let me ride? Maybe I could —"

"Hold on," said Pam. "Let's start at the beginning. Why did you sell Cloud? Was anything wrong with him?"

"Nothing was wrong with him," answered Sandy. "We had to sell him when we sold our farm last year. We sold all of our animals. Except we kept one cat, Toots."

"Why did you sell everything?" asked Anna.

"The farm wasn't making enough money for us to live on," explained Sandy. He rubbed Lightning's upside-down heart marking. "I miss Cloud," he added sadly.

"It's hard to have to sell your pony," said Anna.

"I used to ride Cloud everywhere," continued Sandy. "He's a special pony."

The Pony Pals exchanged a glance. They were all thinking the same thing. Should they tell Sandy what was happening to his special pony?

Lulu nodded. So did Anna and Pam. They all agreed.

Lulu began. She told Sandy that Maggie wasn't a very good pony owner. Anna said that Cloud wouldn't let her touch his face. Lulu added that Maggie was mean.

"My parents wouldn't sell Cloud to a mean person," said Sandy.

"Maggie the Magician fools lots of people," Pam told him. "She must have fooled your parents."

Pam told Sandy about the children's birthday party and how Maggie squirted water in Cloud's face.

Next, Lulu explained that Maggie was trying to sell Cloud. And that Anna pretended she wanted to buy him.

"Lulu pretended the same thing," added Anna.

"But then Maggie found out we are all friends and have our own ponies," said Pam.

"If Maggie doesn't find a new owner for Cloud," concluded Lulu, "she'll sell him for the meat price."

"No way!" exclaimed Sandy. He jumped on his bike. "Where is Cloud? I have to save him."

Pam grabbed Sandy's handlebars to stop him.

"Not so fast," she said. "We need to have a plan. We need some ideas."

"I want to see him," said Sandy. "I *have to.*

What if that awful woman is selling him for meat right now!"

Pam could understand how Sandy felt. "Okay," she told him. "I'll take you to Maggie's. But we have to be careful. We can't let Maggie see us."

"Meanwhile, Anna and I will work on our ideas for saving Cloud," said Lulu.

"Then we'll have a meeting and share our ideas," added Anna. "Lulu and I will wait at the diner for you."

"You should have an idea, too, Sandy," said Lulu. "We'll work together."

Sandy and the girls rode to the diner. Pam tied Lightning to the hitching post with the other ponies.

Anna and Lulu went into the diner. Pam and Sandy took turns running and riding his bike along Belgo Road.

They soon reached Maggie's place.

"Let's hide your bike in the woods," suggested Pam. "Then we'll sneak up to her house."

Pam led Sandy through the woods. "We can hide behind the bushes near the paddock," she whispered to Sandy. "You can see Cloud from there. No matter what happens, stay hidden. Okay?"

"Okay," agreed Sandy. He looked nervous. Pam decided that Sandy Young hadn't done much detective work.

A door slammed.

"It's her!" Pam whispered. "Quick. Duck down and run to the bushes."

Pam bent over and ran behind Sandy. From their hiding place they could see Cloud. He was sleeping standing up. To Pam he looked thinner than ever.

"He looks awful," said Sandy in a loud whisper. "And sad."

Pam put a finger to her lips. "Sh-shh," she warned. "Here she comes."

Maggie was dressed in a bright blue tuxedo and carried Cloud's neck ruffle. She came into the paddock and clipped a lead rope to Cloud's halter.

Cloud woke up, saw Maggie, and tried to pull away from her. But Maggie held him tight.

Pam and Lulu watched as Maggie put the ruffle around Cloud's neck. He shook his head. He doesn't like anything touching his face, thought Pam. Watching Cloud gave her an idea. She took out her notebook and quickly wrote it down.

Maggie led Cloud to the horse trailer. "This is the last party I'm bringing you to," Pam heard her mumble.

Pam tugged on Sandy's arm. "Let's go," she mouthed.

Sandy nodded.

They took turns running and biking back to the diner. As Pam closed the diner door behind them, she saw Maggie's blue truck and horse trailer drive by.

Anna and Lulu were in the Pony Pals' favorite booth. Lulu was writing in a memo pad. Anna's artist notebook was open in front of her. Pam hoped they had some good ideas for saving Cloud.

Four Ideas

Pam and Sandy went to the booth. A plate of brownies and four glasses of milk were on the table.

Pam told Anna and Lulu what they saw at Maggie's. Meanwhile, Sandy borrowed Lulu's pen and quickly wrote his idea on a paper napkin. Then he took a long drink of milk.

"Let's start the meeting," said Pam. "Who wants to go first with their idea?"

"I do," said Sandy.

He handed his napkin to Pam. She read Sandy's idea out loud.

DINER

I WILL BUY CLOUD BACK.

"Do you have enough money to buy a pony?" asked Pam.

"My parents let me keep the money from selling him," explained Sandy. "They said I could buy another pony someday. I want to buy Cloud back now. But where will I keep him?"

"That's where my idea comes in," said Anna. She showed her Pony Pals and Sandy her idea.

"Pam's mother needs help with the riding-school ponies and horses," explained Anna. "Sandy could work for her in exchange for boarding Cloud."

"That's a great idea," said Lulu. "You'd see Cloud every day, Sandy."

"Lightning and Cloud could be together," added Pam. "That would be wonderful."

"Do you have room for another pony at your place?" asked Sandy.

Lulu told Sandy all about the Crandals and their big new barn. "It's a wonderful place for Cloud," she concluded.

"My mom will want to try you out, Sandy," said Pam.

"I took care of the horses and Cloud on our farm," said Sandy. "I know a lot about them."

"What's your idea, Pam?" asked Lulu.

"I'm worried about Cloud's health," said Pam. "My idea is about that."

Pam opened her notebook and put it on the table. Sandy read her idea aloud.

Something is wrong with Cloud's
mouth. Maybe his teeth are bad.
I think that's why he doesn't
want anyone to ride him.

"Or touch his face," added Anna.

"Remember how he spit out the carrot," said Lulu.

"Cloud loves carrots," said Sandy.

"But maybe he can't chew them anymore," said Pam.

"Maggie thinks Cloud is misbehaving," added Anna. "But he might just be in pain."

Sandy put his hand to his cheek. "That's awful," he said.

"What's your idea, Lulu?" asked Anna.

Lulu read her idea to the others.

Dr. Crandal should look at Cloud.

"I thought something might be wrong with Cloud's mouth, too," said Lulu.

"Can your father fix it?" Sandy asked Pam.

"It depends on what the problem is," said Pam thoughtfully. "And how bad it is."

Sandy looked around at the Pony Pals. "Which idea should we do first?" he asked.

"We know that Cloud is safe for the next

few hours," said Lulu. "He's working at a party."

"I want to be there when Maggie comes back," said Sandy. "I want to buy him today."

"What if Maggie has ruined Cloud for riding?" asked Anna. "What if he never lets you ride him again?"

"I don't care," said Sandy. "I still want to save Cloud."

Anna and Pam exchanged a glance. They liked Sandy. He was as crazy about ponies as they were.

Lulu stood up. "Let's go talk to Pam's mother," she said. "I think that's the first step. Then we'll go to Maggie's."

Pam looked at her watch. "It's time for me to do the barn chores, anyway," she said.

"I'll help," said Sandy.

The Pony Pals and Sandy went out to the hitching post.

"Do you want to ride Lightning?" Pam asked Sandy. "I can ride your bike."

"Thanks," said Sandy. He stroked Lightning's neck. "I haven't ridden in a while."

Pam went behind Sandy and Lightning. She saw that Sandy was a good rider. He was steady and gentle with Lightning. And he wasn't a show-off.

While the Pony Pals watered their ponies, Sandy started the barn chores. "Let's keep our ponies saddled," suggested Lulu, "so we're ready to go to Maggie's."

Pam and Anna agreed. They tied their ponies to the hitching post outside the barn. Then they went in to do barn chores with Sandy.

He was cleaning out a stall when Mrs. Crandal came in.

Pam introduced Sandy to her mother.

Sandy told Mrs. Crandal the whole story of what happened to his pony.

"Cloud is the pony you told me about," Mrs. Crandal said to the Pony Pals. "You told me he was a difficult pony."

"He is and he isn't," said Pam.

Everyone started talking at once. They all

wanted to explain why Cloud should be saved.

Mrs. Crandal put up her hand to stop them. "Okay, okay," she said. "Bring Cloud here. We'll try it out."

"Yes!" shouted Anna and Lulu as they hit a high five.

Pam didn't join in the high five. She had a frightening thought. What if Maggie didn't go home after the party? What if she went to sell Cloud?

"He's My Pony!"

Sandy went back into the stall to lay out clean straw. "Let's go to Maggie's the minute we finish," he told the Pony Pals.

"Do you have your money with you?" asked Pam.

Sandy looked up from his work. "It's in the bank," he remembered. "I can get my mom to write a check."

Anna took the rake from him. "Why don't you get it right now?" she said. "We'll finish the stalls."

Sandy ran toward the barn door. "I'll meet

you at Maggie's," he shouted over his shoulder.

An hour later, the Pony Pals halted their ponies in front of Maggie's house.

Pam took the lead up the long driveway. Lightning whinnied softly. "That's right," Pam told her pony. "We're going to see your friend Cloud."

But Cloud wasn't in his paddock. Maggie's truck wasn't there, either.

Lightning looked all around for Cloud. "Cloud will be here soon," she told Lightning. But in her heart, Pam was afraid. They might never see Cloud again.

Anna pulled Acorn up next to Lightning. She looked worried, too. "Maybe they're still working at a party," she told Pam.

Pam dismounted. "Then we'll wait for her," she said.

"I wish Sandy were here," said Lulu.

"I hope he hasn't backed out," added Anna.

As soon as the girls were off their ponies,

they heard a vehicle coming up the driveway. "Here comes Maggie's truck," announced Anna.

But it wasn't Maggie's pickup truck. It was a car. A woman was driving and Sandy Young was in the passenger seat beside her. When they got out of the car, Sandy introduced the Pony Pals to his mother.

"Thank you, girls, for finding Cloud," said Mrs. Young. "We thought we sold him to a good owner."

"Maggie fools people," said Pam.

Just then, Maggie's bright blue truck and the horse trailer came up the drive.

"I hope Cloud is in there," Lulu whispered to Pam.

Lightning whinnied. A faint whinny answered her call. It came from inside the horse trailer.

"Cloud!" shouted Sandy.

Maggie stopped the truck and jumped out. "What's going on?" she shouted angrily. "What are you all doing on my property?"

Mrs. Young stepped forward. "Remember me?" she asked. "My husband and I sold you Cloud."

"Yes," said Maggie. "I remember. So why are you here?"

Pam pointed to Sandy. "He wants to buy Cloud."

"To buy him *back*," said Sandy. "Cloud is my pony."

"What's going on here?" asked Maggie. She glared at Anna and Lulu. "You two said you wanted to buy Cloud, but you already have ponies." She pointed at Pam. "I've had enough of your games."

"It isn't a game," said Pam. "This is serious business. Sandy wants to buy back his pony."

"You told us you were buying Cloud for a pet," said Mrs. Young. "You didn't say that you were using him for a business."

"Or that you were going to neglect him," added Lulu.

"He's in terrible shape," said Anna. "No one can ride him."

"He used to be well trained," said Pam.

Lulu pointed a finger at Maggie. "You don't even like ponies," she accused.

They were all talking at once. Meanwhile, Sandy was getting Cloud out of the horse trailer.

When Mrs. Young saw Cloud, tears came into her eyes. "Poor Cloud," she said softly. She turned to Maggie. "You have neglected that pony," she said.

"We want him back," said Sandy. "We'll give you what you paid for him."

Mrs. Young took out an envelope. "The check is in there. Just sign the bill of sale." Mrs. Young held the envelope and a pen out for Maggie.

"We'll take him right now," added Sandy.

Maggie hesitated for a few seconds. Then she took the envelope. She looked over the check and the bill of sale.

"Okay," she said as she signed her name. "You can have your stupid animal back. He's not good for anything, anyway."

"That's not true," said Pam.

"No one can ride him," said Maggie with a nasty grin.

"We'll see about that," said Pam.

Sandy kissed Cloud's cheek. Cloud pulled away from him.

"Touch him someplace else," Pam told Sandy. Sandy laid his head on Cloud's side. Cloud looked back at him and whinnied softly.

Maggie handed the signed bill of sale to Mrs. Young.

"Get off my property!" shouted Maggie. "Now!"

"How are we getting Cloud to your place?" Sandy asked Pam. "I shouldn't ride him until your father checks his mouth. And I don't want to pull him on a lead rope. That would hurt, too."

"I think Cloud will follow Lightning," said Pam. "You can hold him loosely by the lead rope. That won't hurt."

Pam led Lightning out in front of Cloud and down the driveway. She looked over her shoulder. Cloud was following Lightning.

Lulu and Anna came next on their ponies. Mrs. Young took up the rear in her car. No one said good-bye to Maggie the Magician.

Pam patted Lightning's neck. "We did it, Lightning," she told her pony. "We saved Cloud." Now, she thought, we have to find out what's wrong with his mouth.

She turned around again. Sandy and Cloud were walking side by side. Will Sandy be able to ride his pony again? wondered Pam. Or has Maggie the Magician ruined him forever?

Warm Mash

The parade of ponies and Mrs. Young's car pulled up in front of the Crandals' barn.

"I'll go find your father," said Lulu.

"I'll put our ponies in the paddock," said Anna.

"Let's leave Lightning here with Cloud," suggested Pam.

Mrs. Crandal came out of the barn. Sandy introduced his mother to Pam's mother.

"Thank you for helping us with Cloud," Mrs. Young told Mrs. Crandal. "Your daughter and her friends have been so wonderful."

"The Pony Pals are pretty wonderful," agreed Mrs. Crandal. She walked over to Cloud. "Now let's see what we can do for this poor creature."

Dr. Crandal and Lulu came up to them. Dr. Crandal was carrying his veterinarian bag.

The two mothers, three girls, Sandy, and Lightning stood back while Dr. Crandal examined Cloud.

Dr. Crandal talked to Cloud and touched him on the side. After a few minutes, Dr. Crandal put his hand in Cloud's mouth.

When he took his hand out, he patted Cloud's side again. "You've suffered a lot, buddy," he said.

"What's wrong with him?" asked Sandy.

"Cloud's wolf tooth is loose," Dr. Crandal explained. "The bit hits that tooth. It's been very painful for him."

"Can you fix it, Dr. Crandal?" asked Sandy.

"I'm going to pull the tooth," said Dr.

Crandal. "Cloud doesn't need his wolf tooth and it's causing him a lot of trouble." Dr. Crandal opened his bag and took out a needle. "But first, I'll tranquilize him."

Pam watched while her father gave Cloud a shot in the neck. Anna looked away. She hated needles and shots. But it didn't bother Pam. She wanted to be a veterinarian. Someday she'd have to give shots, too.

Next, Dr. Crandal took out his dental tools and went to work inside Cloud's mouth. Soon the tooth was out. Dr. Crandal held it up for all of them to see.

"It's not very big," commented Anna. "But it caused a big problem."

"I'm going to give him anti-inflammatory drugs," said Dr. Crandal. "His mouth will still be sore for a few more days. He should only have soft food for now. The Pony Pals can keep an eye on him."

"And me," said Sandy. "I'll keep an eye on him, too."

Mrs. Young left to go back to work. Mrs.

Crandal went into the barn to prepare for her next riding lesson. And Dr. Crandal headed back to the animal clinic.

When all of the adults were gone, Pam looked around at Sandy and her Pony Pals. "Let's move Cloud into the stall near my mother's office," she suggested. "It has a little paddock, so he can go in and out."

"Lightning can be in the paddock next to it," suggested Anna.

"And we can make Cloud a warm mash," added Lulu. "We'll make it extra soft and delicious."

Pam led Lightning to the paddock while the others brought Cloud inside. Lightning nickered in Cloud's direction as if to say, "Hey, where are you going?"

"It's all right," Pam told her pony. "You'll see Cloud when he goes into his paddock."

Sandy stayed with Cloud while the Pony Pals made the warm mash.

Cloud was eating when Dr. Crandal came into the barn.

"How's he doing?" he asked.

"Great," said Sandy. "Thank you, Dr. Crandal."

"Will Sandy ever be able to ride Cloud again?" asked Anna.

Dr. Crandal smiled. "Absolutely," he said. "He can ride as soon as Cloud's mouth is healed. The bit won't bother him anymore."

"But Cloud will have to be retrained," said Lulu.

"I don't think so," said Dr. Crandal. "His mouth will feel fine and he will have his old owner back. I think this is a story with a happy ending."

Sandy smiled. "A happy ending thanks to the Pony Pals," he said.

A pony whinnied. Pam looked through the stable door and saw Lightning standing at the fence. Cloud turned and walked out into his paddock.

Lightning and Cloud came on a plane from Ireland together, thought Pam. They were trained together at Echo Farm. Lightning

recognized Cloud at the birthday party. And now they're back together again. It *is* a happy ending, thanks to Lightning.

Cloud and Lightning met at the fence.

"Lightning and Cloud are friends forever," Lulu whispered in Pam's ear. "Just like us."

Dear Reader,

I am having fun researching and writing the Pony Pal books. I've met great kids and wonderful ponies at homes, farms, and riding schools. Some of my ideas for Pony Pal adventures have even come from these visits!

I remember the day I made up the main characters for the series. I was walking on a country road in New England. First, I decided that the three girls would be smart, independent, and kind. Then I gave them their names—Pam, Anna, and Lulu. (Look at the initial of each girl's name. See what it spells when you put them together!) Later, I created the three ponies. When I reached home, I turned on my computer and started to write. And I haven't stopped since!

My friends say that I am a little bit like all of the Pony Pals. I am very organized, like Pam. I love nature, like Lulu. But I think that I am most like Anna. I am dyslexic and a good artist, just like her.

Readers often wonder about my life. I live in an apartment in New York City near Central Park and the Museum of Natural History. I enjoy swimming, hiking, painting, and reading. I also love to make up stories. I have been writing novels for children and young adults for more than twenty years! Several of my books have won the Children's Choice Award.

Many Pony Pal readers send me letters, drawings, and photos. I tape them to the wall in my office. They inspire me to write more Pony Pal stories. Thank you very much!

I don't ride anymore and I've never had a pony. But you don't have to ride to love ponies! And you certainly don't need a pony to be a Pony Pal.

Happy Reading,

Jeanne Betancourt